D0244569

3 8002 02310 323 9

Liquid

NEW MOON   YOUNG   WAXING CRESCENT   WAXING QUARTER   WANING GIBBOUS

FULL   WANING GIBBOUS   WANING QUARTER   WANING CRESCENT   OLD

NEW MOON   YOUNG   WAXING CRESCENT   WAXING QUARTER   WANING GIBBOUS

FULL   WANING GIBBOUS   WANING QUARTER   WANING CRESCENT   OLD

NEW MOON   YOUNG   WAXING CRESCENT   WAXING QUARTER   WAXING GIBBOUS

FULL   WANING GIBBOUS   WANING QUARTER   WANING CRESCENT   OLD

NEW MOON   YOUNG   WAXING CRESCENT   WAXING QUARTER   WAXING GIBBOUS

FULL   WANING GIBBOUS   WANING QUARTER   WANING CRESCENT   OLD

FOR JOEY

Coventry City Council	
CCS	
3 8002 02310 323 9	
Askews & Holts	Oct-2016
	£6.99

Bloomsbury Publishing, London, Oxford, New York, New Delhi and Sydney
First published in Great Britain in 2016 by Bloomsbury Publishing Plc
50 Bedford Square, London, WC1B 3DP

Text & illustrations copyright © Tom Percival, 2016
The moral right of the author/illustrator has been asserted

All rights reserved
No part of this publication may be reproduced or transmitted by any means, electronic,
mechanical, photocopying or otherwise, without the prior permission of the publisher

A CIP catalogue record of this book is available from the British Library

ISBN 978 1 4088 5209 5 (HB)   ISBN 978 1 4088 5211 8 (PB)   ISBN 978 1 4088 5210 1 (eBook)
Printed in China by C & C Offset Printing Co Ltd, Shenzhen, Guangdong

1 3 5 7 9 10 8 6 4 2

www.bloomsbury.com

All papers used by Bloomsbury Publishing are natural, recyclable
products made from wood grown in well-managed forests.
The manufacturing processes conform to the environmental regulations of the country of origin.

BLOOMSBURY is a registered trademark of Bloomsbury Publishing Plc

By the Light of the MOON

TOM PERCIVAL

BEST TOYS

IVan's STUFF

BLOOMSBURY

LONDON OXFORD NEW YORK NEW DELHI SYDNEY

Moving house is a
BIG thing for most people.
And so it was for Ivan . . .

Ivan's old house had always
been so warm and friendly.

This new one was NOT.

It was all so ...

strange.

And his new bedroom
felt strangest of all.

That night, Ivan couldn't sleep.

He stared up at the moon,
just as he *used* to in
the old house.

BOOK

TOYS

And *that* was
when something
unusual happened . . .

A shimmering light drifted down to land in the garden. Ivan's heart fluttered.

What could it be?

He dashed through
the house . . .

and out into the night.

There was the ball of light!
Ivan ran towards it . . .

. . . but the light skipped **away**,

leading him from
rock to stream,

and flower to tree,

until all of a sudden, it vanished.

There was a flash of light
and a small, furry
something appeared.

It had stripes on its tail
and a friendly face.

The creature smiled and wrote its name in the air in large, shining letters.

moji

Then it darted off, painting moonlight *all over* the garden.

Ivan gasped as
the trees grew
ten times taller and
everything came to life.

Then the Moji painted Ivan with moonlight too.

He grew lighter,
and lighter,
and _lighter_,

until . . .

He was flying,
he was *really* flying!

Ivan laughed as they soared up.
Higher than the clouds . . .

higher than the stars . . .

. . . until he could *almost*
touch the moon!

Then they swept back down to earth.
Together they danced through deep forests,
leapt from island to island . . .

and even
explored
underwater.

Ivan had *never* felt so happy.

But all too soon the adventure was over.
The Moji turned to Ivan
and painted one word . . .

ome

"But *this* is not my home,"
said Ivan. "Not *really*."

The Moji smiled
and lit up the sky
with pictures . . .

pictures of Ivan in
the new house.

Happy pictures.

And Ivan understood.
The new house might not
feel like home *yet* . . .

but one day soon
– *it would.*

The Moji nodded and painted one
last word into the sky.

Goodbye

The letters hung there
for a moment until they –
like the Moji – were gone.

NEW MOON   YOUNG   WAXING CRESCENT   WAXING QUARTER   WAXING GIBBOUS

FULL   WANING GIBBOUS   WANING QUARTER   WANING CRESCENT   OLD

NEW MOON   YOUNG   WAXING CRESCENT   WAXING QUARTER   WAXING GIBBOUS

FULL   WANING GIBBOUS   WANING QUARTER   WANING CRESCENT   OLD

NEW MOON   YOUNG   WAXING CRESCENT   WAXING QUARTER   WAXING GIBBOUS

FULL   WANING GIBBOUS   WANING QUARTER   WANING CRESCENT   OLD

NEW MOON   YOUNG   WAXING CRESCENT   WAXING QUARTER   WAXING GIBBOUS

FULL   WANING GIBBOUS   WANING QUARTER   WANING CRESCENT   OLD

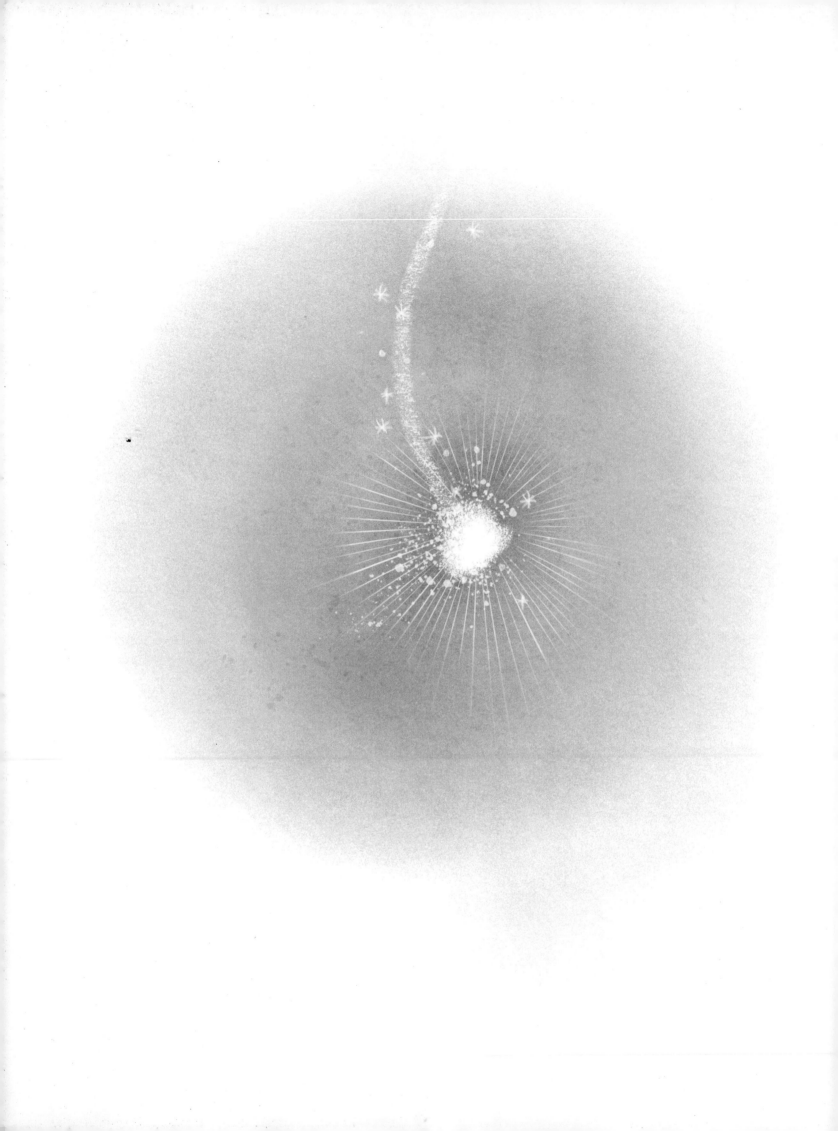